Dedicated to
George and Vi
Richard Berkfield Jr.
Todd, Toni, and Hanna

Printed in the United States of America

ISBN 978-1-60693-863-8

Published by Eloquent Books
An imprint of Strategic Book Group
P.O. Box 333
Durham CT 06422
www.StrategicBookGroup.com

Jake Gets A New Brother

by K. Marie Swift

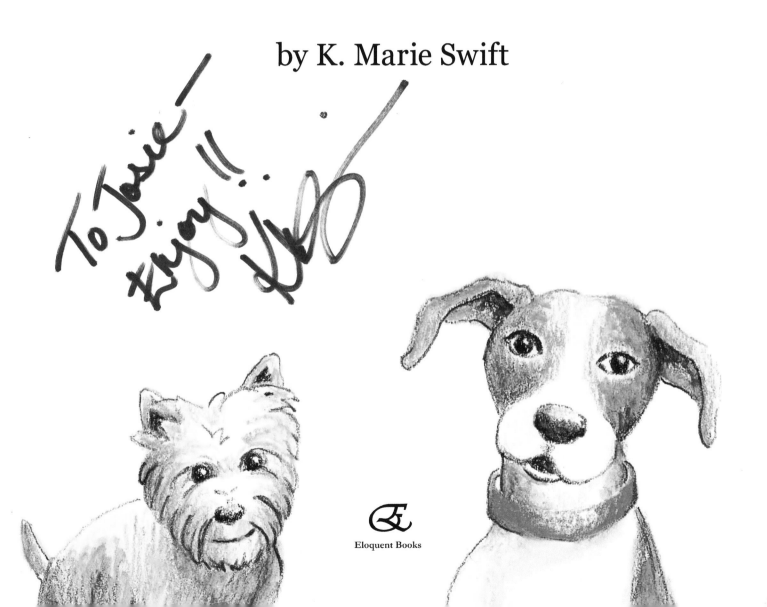

Eloquent Books

For all the four legged teachers in our lives.

My name is Jake and my life has changed forever.

My people brought another dog to live with us. They're even calling him my brother.

I don't want a brother!

Things have been
just fine
around here
without this
brother they've
named *George!*

They seem to have forgotten that I even live here.

4

Making things even worse, he's bigger than me and my people think he's really funny and so cute!

5

I thought if I stayed in my crate and acted really sad they would send him back. So I laid in my crate and acted really sad.

He stayed.

I tried not eating until
they sent him back.

I got
REALLY
hungry.

He stayed.

I tried growling at him
whenever he came near me.

8

He stayed...

...and I got in trouble.

What can I do?

He keeps trying to be my friend by tugging at me to play.

I just want him to *leave me alone!*

My people bought new toys
for us to play with.

I want to play with the new toys
by myself.

Today while we were out in
the backyard, George began
chasing me.

I chased him back.
Hey, that was kind of fun.

Then, George took
one of my toys.

I took one of his toys.

We passed the toys
back and forth...

16

...chasing each other around
and around.

That was fun!

After playing a while,
I heard a familiar voice.
"Jake! George! Here, boys!
It's time for dinner!"

18

George stepped aside as our dinner was set down.

He invited me to eat out of his bowl!

I'm sure glad my people brought me a new brother. George is my new best friend!

The Adventures of Jake and George continues with:

Jake Learns To Swim

Jake And George Have Visitors

Jake And George Meet Their Neighbor

Jake And George Make New Friends

Jake Makes A Difficult Decision

Jake And George Visit The Park